PUFFIN BOOKS

Not Quite a Mermaid

MERMAID TREASURE

Linda Chapman lives in Leicestershire with her family and two Bernese mountain dogs. When she is not writing she spends her time looking after her two young daughters, horse riding and teaching drama.

Not Quite a Mermaid
MERMAID TREASURE

LINDA CHAPMAN

Illustrated by Dawn Apperley

PUFFIN

PUFFIN BOOKS

Published by the Penguin Group
Penguin Books Ltd, 80 Strand, London WC2R 0RL, England
Penguin Group (USA) Inc., 375 Hudson Street, New York, New York 10014, USA
Penguin Group (Canada), 90 Eglinton Avenue East, Suite 700, Toronto, Ontario,
Canada M4P 2Y3 (a division of Pearson Penguin Canada Inc.)
Penguin Ireland, 25 St Stephen's Green, Dublin 2, Ireland
(a division of Penguin Books Ltd)
Penguin Group (Australia), 250 Camberwell Road, Camberwell, Victoria 3124, Australia
(a division of Pearson Australia Group Pty Ltd)
Penguin Books India Pvt Ltd, 11 Community Centre, Panchsheel Park,
New Delhi – 110 017, India
Penguin Group (NZ), cnr Airborne and Rosedale Roads, Albany, Auckland 1310,
New Zealand (a division of Pearson New Zealand Ltd)
Penguin Books (South Africa) (Pty) Ltd, 24 Sturdee Avenue, Rosebank,
Johannesburg 2196, South Africa

Penguin Books Ltd, Registered Offices: 80 Strand, London WC2R 0RL, England

www.penguin.com

First published 2006
1

Text copyright © Linda Chapman, 2006
Illustrations copyright © Dawn Apperley, 2006
All rights reserved

The moral right of the author and illustrator has been asserted

Set in Palatino by Palimpsest Book Production Limited,
Polmont, Stirlingshire
Made and printed in England by Clays Ltd, St Ives plc

British Library Cataloguing in Publication Data
A CIP catalogue record for this book is available from the British Library

ISBN 13: 978–0–141–32054–0
ISBN 10: 0–141–32054–0

www.lindachapman.co.uk

To Sadie Yates, who reminds me of Electra

Contents

Chapter One

'Watch out!' Electra called to Splash, her dolphin. A long dark-blue fish with a sail-like fin on its back came swimming quickly through the gloomy water towards them. Its mouth was open, showing off razor-sharp teeth.

Electra and Splash squeezed against the rocky sides of the tunnel to let it safely past.

'Look how pointy its teeth are,' Splash said.

Electra nodded. 'There are so many weird fish down here. It's really exciting!'

She and Splash were exploring the deepest caves around Mermaid Island. The caves were linked by tunnels that made an underwater maze going all the way out to the deep sea. All sorts of strange creatures lived there. Most of the merpeople who lived on the reef round Mermaid Island avoided the maze, preferring to stay in the shallow, safe waters near the surface. But Electra was different. She loved doing exciting things. Luckily, Splash liked having adventures just as much as she did.

'Come on,' Electra said, her long red

hair swirling about her in the water. 'Let's explore some more.'

Splash whistled anxiously. 'Shouldn't we be getting home? Your mum told us to be back in time for tea and we've been out ages.'

Electra sighed. Splash was right. They *were* late already. 'OK,' she said. 'But let's come back again tomorrow.'

It was easy for them to find their way back through the maze because Electra had placed a ball of mermaid fire in each tunnel. This magic green fire came from the seabed, and Electra had learnt how to collect it in her class at school.

They were just one cave away from the entrance when a tiny purple shape, no bigger than Electra's little finger, came darting through the water towards them. It had a head shaped like a horse, two small horns with two pink spots just below them and a slender curling tail.

'Look, Splash!' Electra exclaimed. 'It's a baby dwarf sea horse!'

Dwarf sea horses were tiny, pretty sea horses with deep-purple bodies that glowed and sparkled like diamonds. They were usually very shy. Electra waited for the baby to dart timidly past them, but it didn't. It stopped and looked at them with bright dark eyes.

Electra put out her hand. The sea horse swam on to her palm. She was astonished. She had never been so close to a dwarf sea horse before.

He opened his mouth as if saying hello.

Electra grinned. 'Hi. I'm Electra.'

The sea horse's little horns wriggled

in a friendly way. Then he darted away from her hand and hid behind a rock.

'I wonder what he's doing on his own like this?' Electra said to Splash. 'I hope he's not lost.'

'We should ask him,' replied Splash.

The sea horse popped up from behind the rock. Electra swam over to it. 'Are you lost?'

Shaking his head, the sea horse whizzed behind a purple-and-red sea cucumber. Electra swam after him but he raced away. She stopped, not wanting to frighten him. Immediately, he stopped too and twitched his horns as if saying, *Come on!*

'I think he wants us to play chase!' Splash exclaimed.

Electra giggled and dived after the sea horse, but there was no way she could keep up with him. He scooted through the water as fast as lightning. Even Splash, who was a very fast swimmer, didn't stand a chance.

'We give up!' Electra panted at last.

The sea horse swam over and looked at them cheekily.

'You're fun,' Electra told him. 'Do you want to be friends with us?'

The sea horse bobbed up and down excitedly. His body glittered like a purple jewel in the water.

'I'll call you Sparkle,' Electra told him. The little sea horse pirouetted in delight.

'Electra!' a cross voice said from behind her.

Electra swung round in surprise. A slim, adult mermaid with long red hair was swimming towards them. 'Mum!' Electra exclaimed. 'What are you doing here?'

'I've been really worried about you,' Maris, Electra's mum, said. 'You told me you'd be home half an hour ago, so I came looking for you and –' She broke off with a gasp as the sea horse dived in front of her nose. 'Oh!' she cried. 'A dwarf sea horse!'

'He's really friendly, Mum. He's been playing chase with me and Splash,' said Electra as the sea horse bobbed around in front of Maris's face. 'He's so cute!' She grinned at the sea horse. 'I've called him Sparkle.'

Sparkle wriggled his horns. Maris's face softened. 'He *is* adorable.

I've hardly ever seen one this close before. He seems very friendly.'

'He is,' Electra agreed. 'I wonder where he lives, Mum?'

'He'll probably live with the other dwarf sea horses,' Maris told her. 'They live together in a secret breeding grotto in this maze. No one knows exactly where it is. Dwarf sea horses swim so fast that no one has ever been able to follow them there.'

'I wish I knew where the grotto was,' Electra said longingly. 'I'd love to see lots of sea horses.'

'Me too,' agreed Splash.

Sparkle darted merrily around the cave.

Maris looked at Electra and Splash. 'Well, cute though Sparkle is, let's say goodbye. It's time for your tea.'

'OK,' Electra said. 'Bye, Sparkle,' she called. 'I hope we see you again.'

The little sea horse bobbed his head as if saying goodbye, and then shot away down the tunnel like a purple arrow.

Electra and Splash followed Maris out of the cave.

Electra kicked hard with her feet to keep up with Maris. Liking adventure

wasn't the only thing
that made Electra
different from the
other merpeople.
While they all had long silver
tails, Electra had legs and feet. This
was because she hadn't been born a
mermaid; she'd been born human. The
merpeople had found her floating in a
small boat after a dreadful storm. She
had been just a tiny baby at the time
and they had rescued her. They had
given her magic sea powder so she
could breathe underwater, and Maris,
who didn't have any children of her

own, had adopted her. Electra was nine now and she couldn't imagine having any other mum, or being anything other than a mermaid.

She put her hand on Splash's fin and let him pull her along through the water. He could swim much faster than Electra could.

Maris smiled at Electra as they swam to the shallower water where the merpeople lived in coral caves.

'Did you two explorers know that there's supposed to be hidden treasure in one of the maze's caves?'

'Hidden treasure?' Electra echoed curiously.

'What treasure?' Splash asked.

'Well, there's an old story I was told at school,' Maris replied. 'It's said that about fifty years ago a ship sank near here. It was carrying gold and jewels. A group of human divers came a little while later to get the treasure back from the wrecked ship. They were in the middle of taking it when another boat of divers came along. The first divers hid the treasure in one of those underwater caves and then there was a fierce battle between the two groups. All of them died and the treasure was left behind.'

'So it's still there?' Electra said, her eyes wide.

'It's certainly never been found,' replied Maris. 'But then it's probably just a made-up story.'

'Oh, wow!' Electra said, imagining treasure chests of gold and jewels piled high in a cave.

Maris saw her face. 'Now, Electra, you've got much more important

things to think about than treasure –
you need to do your homework for
a start. Come along! Hurry up!'
Swishing her tail,
she speeded up.

But Electra hung
back with Splash.
'Did you hear
that, Splash?' she
whispered.

'Yes,' he whistled
excitedly. 'Are we going to
try and find the treasure,
Electra?'

Electra grinned at him. 'Of course!'

Chapter Two

'Treasure!' Sam exclaimed, the following day at school. He and his twin sister, Sasha, were sitting with Electra as they waited for Solon, their teacher, to arrive. They lived in the next-door cave to Electra

and all of them were very good
friends.

'Yes,' Electra told them. 'It's in
the maze!'

'I wonder if there are necklaces
there?' Sasha sighed longingly. 'With
diamonds.' She twirled the
plait in her long blonde
hair and her green eyes
looked dreamy. 'I'd like
a diamond necklace!'

'There are probably
diamonds, sapphires, rubies *and*
emeralds,' Electra said. 'Splash and I
are going to try and find them!'

Sam and Sasha looked very impressed.

'You can come too if you want,' Electra told them.

'What? Into the deep caves?' Sasha said in alarm. 'I wouldn't want to do that!'

Sam, who was braver than his sister, hesitated. 'I don't know. The caves aren't very dangerous. You go in them lots, don't you, Electra?'

Electra nodded. 'It's fun.'

'We *could* go,' Sam said, looking at his sister. 'If we found the treasure we could all share it.' His eyes widened with an idea. 'Why don't we start a treasure hunters' club?'

'Yes!' said Electra in delight.

'You mean have a club with badges and passwords and stuff?' Sasha asked, looking much more interested.

Electra nodded. 'We could all go hunting for the treasure together.'

Nerissa and Hakim, their other friends, swam over to see what everyone was talking about. They were keen to join in too when they heard about the treasure hunters' club.

At breaktime, they each made a badge with a picture of a treasure

chest on it, and then Hakim suggested that they could draw a map. 'We can fill it in as we explore the caves,' he said.

'We've got to think of a password for the club too,' Sasha put in. 'And think about the rules. All clubs have rules.'

While the others wrote down a list of rules, Electra wandered off and looked out towards the deep sea. She couldn't wait until it was the end of school so they could go exploring. She hugged herself tightly.

I hope we find the treasure, she thought.

After school, the five friends and Splash swam down to the caves. They had each brought a bag with them to put treasure in, if they found it. As they reached the maze entrance, Sasha began to look nervous. 'Are you sure it's safe in these caves, Electra?' she asked.

'Of course,' Electra replied. 'I mean,

you have to watch out for the lancet fish, the gulper eels, the viper fish and –'

'What?' Sasha gasped.

Electra caught herself. She didn't want Sasha getting so scared that she wouldn't go exploring. 'Don't worry,' she said quickly. 'You hardly ever see anything dangerous at all.'

It was sort of true. She and Splash had never been hurt by anything in the caves anyway.

They stopped by the maze entrance. Everyone apart from Electra and Splash looked anxious. 'We should all say the password,' Sam suggested.

They bent forward and whispered the password they'd decided on at school. 'Diamonds!'

Electra dived forward eagerly. 'Come on!' she cried.

They swam into the maze. Electra raced quickly through the first few tunnels, taking mermaid fire from the rocks and placing glowing balls of it in every tunnel they went into. It was fun being with the others, even if they did all swim very cautiously and she had to keep stopping to wait for them.

'It . . . it's very creepy in here,' Sasha said in a quavering voice.

'It's quite safe,' Electra told her. 'I promise.' As they reached a turning she hadn't been down before, she felt a rush of excitement. Maybe the treasure was down here! 'Let's go this way!' she called.

'What's that?' Nerissa gasped as a startled fish blew itself up like a spiky ball just in front of them.

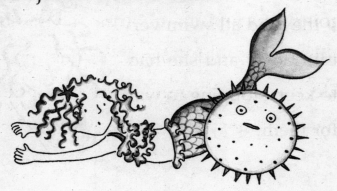

'It's just a pufferfish,' Splash said, nudging her reassuringly. 'Don't worry, Nerissa.'

A stripy blue-and-yellow eel snaked through the water. Sasha squealed as its tail brushed against her. 'I don't like it down here!'

'Maybe we should go back,' Hakim suggested.

But Electra was impatient to keep going and find the treasure. 'Don't be silly,' she told Sasha. 'Come on.' Electra dived round a corner and swam at top speed into a cave.

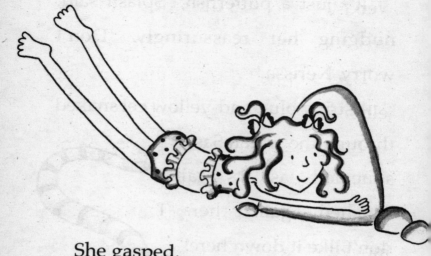

She gasped.

The cave was filled with hundreds of tiny blue-ringed jellyfish.

Electra stopped. Blue-ringed jellyfish had poisonous tentacles and they loved stinging mermaids. 'Go back!' she yelled to the others.

But it was too late. Electra's friends

were already swimming into the cave too.

They stopped dead as they saw the jellyfish.

'Blue-ringed jellyfish!' gasped Sam.

'Help!' shrieked Sasha.

Waving their tentacles, the jellyfish moved in to attack!

Chapter Three

Electra and her friends shrieked as the jellyfish's tentacles swung against their skin. Painful blue circles popped up wherever the tentacles touched.

'My hands!' cried Nerissa.

'My arm!' yelled Hakim.

'My nose!' wailed Sasha as one of the jellyfish stung her on the face. 'Ow!'

'Quick!' Sam began swimming back out of the cave as fast as he could.

'I've been stung all over!' Nerissa exclaimed as they escaped into the tunnel.

Electra looked down at her own skin. Although the others had big blue circles all over them, she just had some faint itchy blotches. It was because the jellyfish's stings didn't affect human skin in the same way that they affected merpeople. Splash's grey dolphin skin seemed OK too.

'I'm sorry,' she said, feeling awful that her mer-friends had been stung so badly. 'I've never seen those jellyfish before. I –'

'You said it was safe down here!' Sasha interrupted. 'You promised!'

'I thought it was,' Electra told her desperately.

'I hate these caves – and all

the horrible creatures in them,' said Nerissa.

'Me too,' declared Sasha. 'My nose really hurts! I'm not going to be a treasure hunter any more. I'm going home!'

'Me too,' said Nerissa.

'No, please wait . . .' Electra began, but the other two girls swam off.

Electra looked at Sam and Hakim. 'I'm really sorry. I wish I could have got to the cave and warned everyone sooner.'

'Well, you didn't,' Sam said crossly, looking at the marks on his arms. 'I'm going home too. I've had enough of treasure hunting for today.'

Hakim nodded and the two of them hurried after the girls.

Electra stared after them in dismay. 'I never meant them to get hurt,' she said to Splash. 'I thought it was safe.' Tears welled in her eyes. She felt terrible that her friends had been stung by the jellyfish. 'Now Sasha doesn't want us to have a treasure hunters' club any more, and I really wanted us all to have adventures together,' she said.

Splash tried to comfort her. 'Maybe Sasha will change her mind.'

'I hope so.' Electra felt too upset to carry on exploring. 'Let's go home now, Splash.'

Splash let Electra hold on to his fin and they began to swim slowly back in the direction of home.

As they passed the cave where the jellyfish had attacked them, Electra

looked in at the blue-ringed jellyfish
that had stung her friends and ruined
everyone's day. Suddenly she frowned.
In the middle of the jellyfish was a tiny
purple shape. Electra tugged at
Splash's fin. 'Stop a minute!'

'What's up, Electra?' Splash
asked.

But Electra was too busy
swimming to the cave entrance
to answer. 'What's that?'
she said curiously,
pointing to the purple
shape.

'I'm not sure,'

Splash said, joining her. 'It looks like . . . it looks like . . .'

'It's Sparkle!' Electra cried as she made out a small tail curling fearfully above a head with two pink spots. It was the baby sea horse from the day before. His dark eyes were wide with fright.

'The jellyfish are about to attack him!' Splash exclaimed.

Electra's hand flew to her mouth. 'Oh, Splash! We've got to do something!'

Chapter Four

As the jellyfish's tentacles swung towards Sparkle, Electra dived forward bravely. She knew she was going to get stung again but she didn't care. She had to rescue him!

Splash plunged into the cave beside

her. 'I'm coming too! I'll push the jellyfish out of the way with my nose. You get Sparkle!'

'OK!' Electra exclaimed.

Splash whooshed forward, his grey face butting into the shoal of jellyfish. They flipped through the water, twirling and tumbling as he swept his nose from side to side. Diving past him, her heart pounding, Electra grabbed Sparkle in her outstretched hands. She felt several jellyfish sting her but she didn't turn back.

'It's OK,' she murmured, pulling the little sea horse close to her chest.

'I've got you. You're going to be all right.'

Turning round, Electra kicked hard with her feet and swam out of the cave. With a last wave of his head that scattered the jellyfish all over the place, Splash followed her.

They stopped when they were a safe distance away. Electra opened her

hands and Sparkle swam out. Swimming up to Electra's face, he wound his tail round a strand of her hair and nuzzled her cheek. He opened and shut his mouth. Electra smiled. She was sure he was saying thank you.

'I'm just glad we could help you,' she told him, scratching the new marks on her arms. They were itchy but she didn't care. All that mattered was that Sparkle was safe. 'What were you doing in there on your own?' she asked him. 'You should be safe with your family.'

Sparkle danced away through the water. He looked back over his shoulder, his eyes glinting cheekily.

Splash grinned. 'Perhaps he's like you and me, Electra. Perhaps he just likes having adventures!'

Electra smiled as Sparkle nodded at Splash's words before darting towards a tunnel. 'I think you're right.'

The little sea horse twirled round and vanished.

When Electra and Splash got back to the underwater cave where they lived with Maris, they saw Sasha and the others in the garden of the next-door cave. Sasha was choosing a sea lettuce for tea. Her nose still had a big blue ring on it. 'What's everyone going to say when I go to school looking like this tomorrow!' she was wailing. 'They'll all laugh at me!'

'Hi!' Electra called.

Her friends looked round, but when they saw it was Electra they just frowned. Sasha turned her back.

Electra's heart sank. These were her best friends. She hated them being cross with her. 'I'm really sorry, everyone,' she said, swimming over and stopping beside a patch of pink and lilac anemones. 'I  thought the caves were safe. I wish you hadn't been stung. I didn't mean it to happen. I'm so, so sorry.'

Sam hesitated and then sighed. 'It's OK, Electra.'

'Yeah, I guess the stings don't itch that much any more,' Hakim said.

Nerissa nodded in agreement. 'You didn't know the jellyfish were there. It wasn't really your fault.'

Sasha didn't say anything. She still looked very upset.

Electra felt awful. She swam over to her. 'I wished you'd stayed, Sasha,' she said softly, looking at her friend. 'Splash and I saw this really cute dwarf sea horse. You'd have loved him.'

Sasha looked interested despite herself. 'Really? You actually saw a dwarf sea horse?'

Electra nodded. 'He was being attacked by the jellyfish.' She quickly told the others what had happened.

'So you and Splash had to swim

right into the jellyfish to rescue him!'
Sam gasped.

'That was really brave of you both,'
Sasha said, her eyes wide.

Electra shrugged. 'We couldn't have
left him there.'

Splash shook his head. 'We had to
rescue him.'

'He's so cute and very friendly,'
Electra went on. 'He's not at all shy.'

'I wish I could see him,' Sasha said
longingly.

'Me too,' agreed Nerissa.

'Well, if you come back into the
caves, maybe you might,' Electra said.

The others all looked at each other.

'Oh, please,' Electra begged them. 'Please say you'll all stay in the treasure hunters' club. We might see the sea horse again and we still might find the treasure!'

'All right,' said Sam, Hakim and Nerissa.

Sasha hesitated.

'Sasha?' Electra asked.

'Well, I'll only be in the club if you agree to be extra careful. If there's anything dangerous at all, we can come straight back.' Sasha looked warily at Electra. 'Do you promise?'

Electra nodded. 'Promise.'

'And we won't do *anything* dangerous,' Sasha said.

'No,' Electra agreed.

Sasha smiled at her. 'Then I'll stay in the treasure hunters' club.'

'Shall we go looking for treasure again tomorrow when you finish school?' Splash asked eagerly.

Everyone nodded.

Just then, Maris pushed aside the cockle-shell curtains that hung across the doorway of their cave. 'Electra! Splash! Teatime!'

'Coming, Mum!' Electra called. She and Splash swam towards Maris. Electra felt very excited. She couldn't wait until they all went looking for treasure again!

After school the next day, Electra and the others headed straight for the maze, carrying their bags.

'Password!' Sasha said as they reached the entrance cave.

'Diamonds!' they all whispered.

Electra plunged off with Splash but Sasha flicked her tail and swam up in front of them, stopping them in their tracks.

'We're not going in till we've got the rules clear,' she said, looking firmly at Electra. 'The first rule is that we have to go very slowly and the second rule is that we have to stop at every corner and check there's no danger ahead of us.'

'I think we should say the password every time we stop,' Nerissa put in.

Electra thought it sounded a bit boring but when she saw everyone else nodding, she nodded too.

'Can we go now?' she asked.

'Yes,' Sasha said, looking much happier.

They all set off into the tunnel. Everyone swam very slowly. Electra could feel her stomach curling up with impatience as they dawdled along. At this rate, they were never going to reach the deeper caves where the treasure might be.

'We don't have to stop to say the password at *every* corner,' she said, after Sasha had made them stop for the fourth time.

'Yes, we do. It's the rules,' Sasha said.

'The rules are boring!' Electra complained.

'You promised,' Sasha reminded her.

Electra sighed impatiently and they swam on.

Luckily, this time they saw nothing scary at all. They swam deeper into the caves.

'We could be really near the treasure now,' Electra whispered to Splash. 'The water feels colder here, which means we must be getting near the deep sea.' She dived down to the floor to leave another ball of mermaid fire marking the way, then added, 'And we haven't been in these tunnels before.'

Splash clicked his tongue excitedly. 'We might be very near where the ship was wrecked.'

As he spoke, one of his flippers brushed against the bottom of the tunnel. In the glow of the green mermaid fire something glinted!

'Splash! Look!' Electra exclaimed.

She swooped down and grabbed the glittering object from the sand. It was a large gold coin!

Chapter Five

'Treasure!' Electra gasped, holding up the coin and looking at Splash in delight. 'We've found a piece of treasure! Quick!' she called to Sam, Sasha, Nerissa and Hakim. 'Splash and I have found something!'

The others swam
over.

'Wow!' said Sam,
staring at the coin in
Electra's hand.

'Are there any more coins?' Hakim
asked.

'No,' Electra replied, checking in the
sand. 'Just this one.'

'Maybe the divers dropped it when
they were hiding the rest of the
treasure,' Sam suggested.

Nerissa clutched Sasha's arm. 'That
might mean the treasure's near here.'

'Let's look!' cried Electra.

Everyone, apart from Sasha, raced off down the tunnel at top speed.

'Wait!' Sasha shouted. 'You're breaking the rules!'

They all stopped and swung round.

'We could be about to find the treasure, Sasha!' Electra exclaimed impatiently. 'The rules don't matter!'

'Yes, they do,' Sasha argued. She looked round nervously. 'We don't want to get into trouble again.'

'We won't. Come on!' Electra urged her.

Sam, Hakim and Nerissa nodded, but Sasha frowned. 'No, we all agreed.

We *have* to swim slowly and stop at every corner.'

'But that's silly,' Electra said. 'Let's just go and find the treasure.'

'No!' Sasha swished her tail angrily.

Electra began to lose her temper. 'You're being stupid!'

'I'm not!' Sasha cried.

'Stop arguing, you two,' Sam protested, but Electra and Sasha ignored him.

'You're ruining everything, Electra!' Sasha shouted.

'I'm not the one who's ruining everything,' Electra said. 'You are.

This is supposed to be a treasure hunters' club. Why don't you go home if you're too scared to be in it!'

'Fine!' Sasha snapped. 'I don't want to be in your stupid club anyway!' Turning round, she swam off but she was so upset that she forgot to follow the glow of the mermaid fire.

Electra saw Sasha turn into the wrong tunnel.

'Sasha, wait!' she cried. 'That's not the way home.'

But Sasha was crying too hard to hear Electra and she didn't stop.

'She'll get lost, Electra,' Nerissa said anxiously.

'I'll go after her,' Electra said. She charged down the tunnel. 'Sasha! Come back!'

But Sasha was a fast swimmer and there was no sign of her. Electra raced on. At last, she caught sight of Sasha's silver tail plunging into a cave up ahead.

'That's the wrong way!' Electra

yelled. Swimming as fast as she could, she dived into the cave after Sasha.

To her relief, Sasha had stopped. There were six tunnels leading off the cave and Sasha was looking at them anxiously. Seeing Electra come into the cave, her face flooded with relief. 'Electra! I thought I was lost. I forgot to follow the mermaid fire.'

'I've been following you,' Electra gasped. 'You shouldn't have swum off like that. It could have been really dangerous.'

Sasha hung her head. 'I know. It was a stupid thing to do. I was just cross because you weren't following the rules and I think . . . well, I was a bit scared because we're so deep in the caves. I'm sorry, Electra. I shouldn't have shouted at you and said you were ruining everything. Thank you for coming after me. Can we be friends again?'

'Of course.' Electra swam forward and hugged her. 'I'm sorry we argued too. I shouldn't have told you to go home. It's just that I wanted us to find the treasure so much.' Her eyes shone. 'Oh, Sasha, imagine how exciting it would be if we did find it!'

Sasha looked happier. 'Yeah!'

'Let's go back to the others and keep looking,' Electra said.

Sasha nodded. 'Which tunnel is it? I've forgotten which one I came down.'

Electra glanced behind her. There were three identically gloomy tunnels. 'I think it's the one in the middle,' she said, but then she hesitated. 'No, hang on, I'm sure I remember passing that clump of tubeworms,' she said, looking at a large bush of white and red tubeworms in the entrance to the left-hand tunnel.

'There are tubeworms in that one as well,' Sasha said, pointing to the tunnel on the right.

'It must be . . .' Electra trailed off. 'I don't know,' she said in a small voice.

Sasha stared at her with frightened eyes. 'What are we going to do?'

Electra gulped. 'We must be able to work it out.' She swam to the tunnel on the right. It was dark inside. She went a little way in.

Swoosh! A black gulper eel, with an enormous gaping mouth, swept out of the dark straight towards her.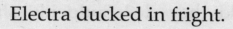

Electra ducked in fright.

Sasha squealed as it shot past her and disappeared down one of the other tunnels. 'Oh, Electra!' she gasped. 'I'm scared!'

Electra swam back to her. 'Don't worry,' she said, trying to be brave but feeling close to tears. How were they *ever* going to find their way back to the others? If they went down the wrong tunnel they might end up getting even more lost. Maybe so lost that no one would *ever* find them.

Sasha started to cry.

Electra looked around desperately. What could they do? Suddenly she saw a tiny purple shape bobbing out of one of the tunnels.

It was a dwarf sea horse.

Electra stared at the two pink spots on its head. 'Sparkle!' she cried. She grabbed Sasha's arm. 'Sasha, it's the sea horse I was telling you about.'

Sasha looked up as the tiny sea horse danced over.

He looked at them with his head on one side. His eyes darted from Electra to Sasha, who was brushing her tears away. Electra was sure that if he could talk, he would have been asking her what was wrong.

'We're lost, Sparkle,' she told him. 'We don't know the way home. Do you?' she asked hopefully.

Sparkle nodded.

'You do?' Electra cried.

Sparkle nodded again and then swam to the left-hand tunnel. He stopped as if waiting for them to follow.

Electra gasped. 'Sasha! I think Sparkle knows the way home.'

Sasha's eyes widened.

The little sea horse wriggled his horns.

'Let's follow him!' Electra said.

Chapter Six

Electra and Sasha swam after Sparkle. The tunnel was dark and winding, and sharp rocks jutted out of the roof. 'I'm sure this wasn't the tunnel we came down,' Electra said after a while.

'Maybe it's a short cut,' Sasha said hopefully.

Sparkle zoomed on, turning round occasionally to check that they were still following.

The water began to feel much colder.

'Brrr,' Electra said, shivering.

Sasha frowned. 'Shouldn't the water be getting warmer if we're getting closer to Mermaid Island?'

Electra nodded. 'Sparkle!' she called out as the sea horse darted round the corner in front of them. 'This is the right way, isn't it?' She followed him. 'You are taking us home and . . . Oh!' She broke off with a gasp as she stopped in the entrance to a cave.

Sasha almost bumped into her. 'What is it? What's . . . Oh, wow!' She gasped too.

They were standing in an underwater grotto that seemed to be glowing with a strange golden light. Hundreds of sea horses bobbed, ducked and dived through the water. Seeing the two mermaids, they stopped and stared in surprise.

'Dwarf sea horses!' Electra took a deep breath, hardly able to believe her eyes. 'Lots of them!'

Clumps of feathery pink and green seaweed grew up from the floor, waving in the golden water. Around them danced other sea horses, who looked even tinier. 'Babies!' Electra exclaimed.

'This must be the sea horses' breeding grotto,' Sasha said. 'I can't believe we've found it, Electra!'

'It's not the only thing we've

found.' Electra stared at the floor of the cave. 'Look!'

On the floor of the grotto were five old wooden treasure chests. Gold coins and jewellery spilt out of them on to the floor.

Sasha gasped. 'It's the lost treasure! That's what's making the water look so golden!'

Electra dived to the floor. There were necklaces, bracelets, rings and

even a diamond brooch in the shape of a sea horse, with sapphires for eyes. Baby sea horses were dancing around the jewels, playing hide-and-seek and chase.

'This is where the divers hid it,' Electra said.

Being careful not to disturb any of the tiny sea horses, Electra picked up a handful of necklaces and coins. 'We've got to take something home to show everyone,' she said, putting the treasure into the bag she was carrying.

'Otherwise they'll never believe us!' She picked up the sea-horse brooch. The diamonds shone.

'Um, Electra,' Sasha said slowly, 'how *are* we going to get home?'

Electra frowned. She'd been so amazed to see the treasure and the sea horses' grotto that she'd forgotten they were lost.

Sparkle bobbed over to them. 'Oh, Sparkle!' Electra exclaimed as she realized what must have happened. 'I bet you thought that when we said we wanted to go home, we wanted to come here – to *your* home – didn't you?'

Sparkle nodded.

'But we wanted to go back to *our* home,' Electra told him. Her heart sank. They might have found the treasure *and* the secret sea-horse grotto, but it looked as if they were just as lost as ever!

Sasha seemed to realize the same thing. 'What are we going to do? How are we ever going to get back?'

Sparkle darted upwards. He seemed to be talking to the other sea horses. They began to nod, and then slowly and cautiously they swam down to the two mermaids. 'What's happening?' Sasha said as the sea horses surrounded them in a dancing purple cloud.

Sparkle bobbed in front of Electra's nose, then, twining his tail in her hair, he pulled.

Electra didn't know what to do. He pulled again more insistently.

'I think he wants us to go with them,' Electra said.

Sparkle nodded and pulled again.

'Let's do it,' Sasha said.

Electra and Sasha began swimming. The sea horses darted and dived around them. With their glittering bodies to light the way, the tunnel didn't seem gloomy at all. Electra and Sasha flipped themselves on to their backs. There were sea horses like purple jewels everywhere.

Sasha laughed. 'This is fun!'

They swooshed through the rocky tunnel, and out into the cave they had been lost in. Sparkle led the way into the middle tunnel. It twisted and turned and then suddenly they saw the glow of green mermaid fire in a tunnel ahead of them.

'We're near the others!' Electra cried. As they turned into the tunnel, there was a chorus of exclamations and cries. Splash, Sam, Nerissa and Hakim were waiting, and with them were Maris and Ronan, the twins' dad.

'Electra! Where have you been?' Maris exclaimed.

'Mum!' Electra said in shock. 'What are you doing here?'

The sea horses swooped up to the ceiling as Maris swam forward and hugged Electra in relief. 'Splash came to find me. He said you and Sasha were lost in the caves. I told Ronan and we followed your balls of mermaid fire until we found the others. But they didn't know where you'd gone.'

'We've been very worried about you,' Ronan said, hugging Sasha.

'We thought you'd be lost forever,' Nerissa said in a shaking voice.

'We might have been,' replied Electra. 'But the sea horses helped us to find our way back.'

Everyone looked up at the tiny sea horses darting about the roof of the cave like jewels in the water. 'There are so many of them!' Ronan said. 'Where have they all come from?'

'Oh, Dad,' Sasha said, her eyes shining. 'We found the sea horses' breeding grotto.'

'And the treasure too!' Electra burst out, holding up the bag of treasure she was carrying.

'What?' everyone shrieked.

'It's hidden in the sea horses' grotto,' she said.

It didn't take long for Electra and Sasha to explain.

'What shall we do?' Electra asked anxiously as they finished. 'If we move the treasure, it will disturb the sea horses.'

'And the water won't be so pretty for them any more,' Sasha added.

Maris looked at Ronan.

He rubbed his chin. 'We'll have to talk to the other merpeople back at the reef, but I think it should stay in the grotto. We can keep this treasure you've brought in your bag and the rest could remain with the sea horses. It's good to know that it's been found after all these years, but we don't need it.'

Electra was surprised. 'But it's treasure!'

'I know,' Maris said, taking her hand. 'But Ronan's right. After all, we don't need human gold.' She looked at the dancing, darting sea horses and smiled. 'We have our own living treasure in the sea.'

Electra looked at the cloud of tiny, bright-eyed creatures with their glittering bodies and knew her mum was right. No jewels could ever be as beautiful as the dancing sea horses.

'You and Sasha do deserve a reward, though, for finding the treasure,' Maris went on.

'It was Electra really,' Sasha said

loyally. 'If she hadn't come after me when I swam off, I'd have been lost in the caves on my own. And she knew that Sparkle was telling us to follow him.'

'Can we all choose something, Mum?' Electra asked. 'Sam, Nerissa and Hakim as well? After all, we're in the treasure hunters' club together and it wouldn't be fair if just Sasha and I got something.'

Hakim, Sam and Nerissa grinned at her.

'All of you,' agreed Ronan, holding out the bag. 'Come and choose.'

They swam over eagerly. Sasha took a diamond necklace, Nerissa chose an emerald bracelet, and Sam and Hakim wanted matching gold coins studded with rubies. When it was her turn, Electra didn't hesitate. She took out the small sea-horse brooch. The diamonds and sapphires on it shone in the water as she held it in her hand.

Sparkle dived forward to look at it curiously. Electra reached out and stroked him. 'It'll remind me of you,' she told him softly as he wound his tail round her finger.

Near the ceiling of the tunnel, the other sea horses swirled together in a group.

Maris put her arm round Electra. 'I think it's time to say goodbye.'

'Bye, Sparkle,' Electra whispered.

Sparkle nuzzled her cheek. Above them, the other sea horses began to stream away down the tunnel. Sparkle unwound his tail from Electra's finger, then, giving her a last cheeky look, he darted after his friends and family.

Within seconds, he was swallowed up in the glittering, glowing purple cloud.

Electra hugged Maris. 'I hope Sparkle keeps having adventures.'

Maris smiled. 'Oh, I think he will.'

Splash nudged Electra's arm. 'Just like us, Electra.'

She grinned at him. 'Just like us!'

Do you love magic, unicorns and fairies?

Join the sparkling

Linda Chapman

fan club today!

It's FREE!

You will receive a sparkle pack, including:

Stickers
Membership card

Badge
Glittery pencil

Plus four Linda Chapman newsletters every year,
packed full of fun, games, news and competitions.
And look out for a special card on your birthday!

How to join:

Visit lindachapman.co.uk and enter your details

Send your name, address, date of birth* and email address (if you have one) to:
Linda Chapman Fan Club, Puffin Marketing,
80 Strand, London, WC2R 0RL

Your details will be kept by Puffin only for the purpose of sending information regarding Linda Chapman
and other relevant Puffin books. It will not be passed on to any third parties.
You will receive your free introductory pack within 28 days

*If you are under 13, you must get permission from a parent or guardian

Notice to parent/guardian of children under 13 years old: Please add the following to their email/letter includin
your name and signature: I consent to my child/ward submitting his/her personal details as above.